ENCHANTING ELAINE
HOWLING FOREST SHIFTERS PREQUEL

BETH DEWEESE

Editing by Andie Smith & Nova Jarvis

Cover Design by Getcovers

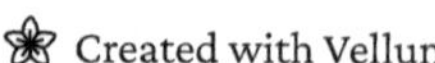 Created with Vellum

This story is for all the readers living their epilogue. Ever after is a long time to keep the love alive, but a little spice can go a long way.

CHAPTER 1
ELAINE

Elaine was cleaning out the fridge. Because it was Tuesday, and she always cleaned out the fridge on Tuesdays.

She tried to mix it up once. Got really crazy and waited until Friday. Hooboy, that was a spectacular failure.

Her husband and sons began complaining of the smell by Thursday. Wolf shifters had an excellent sense of smell, even in human form. And her little pack of wolves could not stand the smell of her attempt to add a little variety into her week.

So, Tuesdays it was.

She collected all the raw meat and carried it into the garage to place in the deep freezer. The family was leaving on a royal visit to the Byrne pack later that day, and the meat wouldn't keep until they returned. So, this Tuesday's clean-out was extra thorough.

Elaine lifted the lid to the freezer and looked at the tidy little stacks of meat packages, all labeled precisely with date and type of meat. Everything in neat rows and columns, organized and waiting for crock-pot Mondays. Or maybe Thursdays, when her husband, the king, liked to grill steaks.

Feeling inspired, she tossed her handful into the freezer and let the packages fall where they may. A satisfying *thunk* accompanied the toppling of several columns of frozen meat. She stood, admiring her handiwork, until the guilt hit her. She really shouldn't leave things in disorganized shambles like this.

Elaine bent over to undo her rebellion and restore order. As she felt around the frozen packages, her fingers felt the cold of the deep freeze. It was painful, but she had almost removed all traces of chaos when she felt something fuzzy. The texture felt different from the cuts of meat frozen in brown paper wrappers, enough so that it sparked her curiosity.

She pulled the incongruous package out and closed the lid to the freezer. She instantly recognized what it was: a felt jewelry box containing either a bracelet or a necklace. Given the length of the rectangle, most likely a necklace.

Her heart rate kicked up. *Why would Theo put a necklace in the bottom of the deep freezer?* Her gut knew she had accidentally stumbled onto a hiding place.

Which could have any number of innocent explanations. Her mind flipped through a Rolodex of possibilities.

But her birthday wasn't for another six months.

And they just finished the Christmas holiday.

Their mating anniversary was still over a month away, and they had a big celebration last year for their seventieth anniversary. She expected nothing much this year for their seventy-first.

Her hands trembled as she opened the jewelry box. A diamond pendant sparkled, with smaller rubies along the chain twinkling in the light. It was stunning...but also unlike any piece of jewelry she owned. She had several sets of royal jewels, but they were all understated compared to this beauty. And all the royal jewels formed sets, with matching earrings, bracelets, rings, necklaces. Many of them coordinated with one of her crowns or tiaras.

This necklace was unlike any of them.

It was a striking style, bold in a way her other jewelry was not.

Bold in a way *she* was not.

Was this necklace meant for someone *else*? Elaine's heart began to race at the thought that she had discovered Theo's hiding spot for gifts meant for another woman. Had he finally gotten bored with her?

The sound of the front door closing reminded her the kids would be home soon to finish packing. She snapped the box closed in a loud clap, and she couldn't help a flinch. Panicking, she returned the necklace to its original hiding spot and hurried back into the kitchen.

She sniffed back her tears before her daughter, Theodora, bounded into the house. Her thoughts were spiraling around worst-case scenarios, but she didn't want her children to see her turmoil.

"Mama! Mama, where are you? Mamaaa!" Theodora was calling without giving her a chance to respond.

"I'm in here, baby. Come to the kitchen."

The hustle and bustle of her arriving family quickly enveloped Elaine. Theo trailed behind their daughter, and her sons Jack and Declan followed him. Everyone was hungry for a snack, and Elaine used the flurry of activity to avoid Theo's eyes.

She kept her focus on preparing an assortment of snacks from the food that was left in the fridge while Theodora recounted their entire day in great detail.

Her hand held a knife, about to slice an apple, when Theo's palm covered hers, stilling her movement.

"Hello, mate." Theo was behind her, and he used his free hand to tilt her chin for a kiss. She puckered her lips for a peck, but he wanted more than that. His palm slid up her cheek, and he pressed her lips for entry.

All worries and doubt melted from Elaine as she reciprocated the now passionate kiss. As Theo's tongue pushed into hers, he pushed away her worry. Theo loved her. They were happy. He wouldn't be disloyal to his mate.

"Eww, gross!" Declan scrunched his nose and stuck out his tongue.

"Yuck! Stop that, you guys!" Jack chimed in. "I'm going upstairs. I lost my appetite."

Theo leaned back from her at the chorus of complaints from their teenagers. Still wrapped around her back, Theo addressed them.

"You kids will eat the snack your mamma is preparing for you. And you'll watch your tone. I'll kiss my mate whenever and wherever I want, and you three should be so lucky to have a mate like your mama one day." Theo made eye contact with each child one by one. Theodora watched their interaction with interest, but the boys recognized his tone and knew grumbling would only get them in real trouble.

After a moment, Theo released Elaine to load suitcases into the car. The rest of the day was a flurry of activity getting two teenage boys and their baby sister mobilized to leave on time to make their flight.

As they sat at the gate, waiting for time to board their flight, Theo took her hand in his and placed it on his thigh.

"Tell me what has you so distracted, love. You haven't said two words in a row to me since we left the house."

Theo used his free hand to place a lock of her hair behind her ear.

"It's fine. I mean, I'm fine. It's nothing. There is nothing." She shook her head to clear the jumble of words. He would never believe her if she didn't sound totally normal.

"I don't believe you." Now Theo was nuzzling her hair. "Out with it."

Elaine exhaled and looked around at all the humans surrounding them in the airport. "It really is nothing, dear. But maybe we should talk about this later, hmm?"

"I'll leave you to your secrets for now. But don't think this reprieve will be indefinite." He was using his king's voice with her now. Whatever, she knew there wasn't any real threat behind it. Not with her, anyway.

But why did he bring up the topic of secrets? Was he projecting onto her?

Her mind couldn't help but think back to one of her mom's boyfriends. After her mate and Elaine's father died, she went through a succession of boyfriends, each worse than the last. Number Three liked to project whenever he was hiding something. He would accuse her mom of lying when really it was he who told the lie. Was Theo doing that to her?

"Mama, I don't like flying with the hu—" Theodora interrupted her thoughts with a whine, but Elaine quickly shushed her.

"Baby, you can't talk like that, remember? We fly with *other people* because this is a short trip to visit our friends, and we don't need to spend the money on a private jet for an easy journey like this." Elaine used the opportunity to disentangle from Theo and let her daughter sit on her lap. She started braiding her hair to distract her from the wait.

"Did you at least get us first-class tickets?" Jack asked.

"Yes, son. I did," Theo answered.

Both Declan and Jack made exaggerated *phew* gestures, then they all descended into giggles.

Before long, the family boarded the plane. Elaine subtly maneuvered the children to separate herself from Theo.

A cross expression from Theo let her know he knew what she was about, but he was letting it slide.

Oh, well. He could be cross. It was a short flight, and she needed a little space to collect her thoughts. She knew he was loyal. He was a good mate and a good father.

As Theodora fidgeted in her seat, she took out a couple interior design magazines she had stuffed in her bag.

"Theodora, help mama pick out new furniture for the house." Elaine opened the first magazine on her tray table in such a way that Theodora could see it, too.

"Are you redecorating? Our house? Why?" Declan asked from her other side.

"Oh, you know. Our house has looked the same for years now. Since your father and I...came together. I thought maybe it would be fun and exciting to have a change. Mix things up a little bit." Declan did not look convinced that this was a good idea. So, she flipped to a page she had doggie eared. "Look at this Declan. Wouldn't it be so great if our living room looked like this?" She held up the magazine.

"Maybe, I guess. But why change anything? Everything is just fine the way it is now. I finally made my spot on the couch have a perfect butt print on the cushion." Declan looked proud of himself.

"No way, that spot is at least half shaped from my butt. That isn't just your butt print, Declan!" Jack was leaning over Declan to talk to her.

"We can keep the couch, boys, if your butt print is that

important to you. But wouldn't you like to see something different, too? Like, maybe a new rug or different curtains?" Elaine looked from one child to another in search of support.

"I think that's a great idea, mama. I'll help you pick out something pretty." Ah, her favorite child answered.

"Thank you, Theodora. You see? That's how you're supposed to treat your mother. You think all her ideas are wonderful." She elbowed Jack a couple times, and both brothers rolled their eyes.

Theo observed his family's antics silently. She did not prod him for input, but she knew how sharp he was. She decided not to think about Theo at all as she and Theodora carefully studied the design possibilities in the magazines she brought.

A visit with her friend couldn't come at a better time. Talking things over with Liv during their trip would help her sort out her scattered thoughts.

CHAPTER 2
ELAINE

Later that day, after their arrival at the royal residence of the Byrne pack and after dinner with the royal family, the adults were relaxing around a bonfire while the kids entertained themselves inside the house.

It had been a long day, with the travel and the worry Elaine carried in the back of her mind. Getting everyone settled and ready for dinner had kept her thankfully occupied since their arrival. No more of Theo's observant gaze studying her facial expression and interaction. She knew he could tell she was worried about something, but she wasn't ready to confront him over the necklace.

Every time she pictured the necklace in that cold, velvet box, her mind couldn't resist comparing the moment to the memory of her mother discovering a pair of diamond earrings in their kitchen. Just like this morning, Elaine's mother had been cleaning out the fridge and found the earrings stashed in the back corner of the freezer. She had just come home from school as her mother was confronting Number Four about her discovery.

Was history repeating itself?

Theo was nothing like Number Four. Or any of them.

But what are the chances that two generations of her family would catch a cheater by finding jewelry in the freezer? Who even does that? No one stores fine jewelry in the freezer unless they are hiding something.

A log crackled and broke apart, sending a flurry of sparks flying with a pop. Queen Olivia, Liv as Elaine knew her, put her arm around Elaine's shoulders.

"Where did you go? Your mind was worlds away," Liv whispered.

Elaine couldn't help darting a glance at Theo, sitting on the opposite side of the fire. "I'm fine."

Liv didn't push, and her oblivious husband changed the subject before Theo could say anything.

"How are your children doing? Jack seems to have hit a bit of a growth spurt." Harold said.

"Growing strong and healthy, thankfully. Declan is fifteen now, and he's begging us to let him get his learner's permit so he can start driving. I don't think we can put him off much longer." Theo chuckled as he rubbed the stubble growing on his jaw.

"I can't believe humans let their children drive at such a young age. The thought of my child driving a vehicle terrifies me, and wolf pups are much heartier than human children." Harold shook his head. "We haven't let Johnny drive amongst the humans yet. We still limit him to driving on family lands."

"It's the only thing Harry and I argue about," Liv said.

"My mate would have the kids live just like the humans. She doesn't see how bad an influence human culture is on impressionable wolf pups. Yes, we must learn enough to blend in and assimilate. But that doesn't mean we have to raise our pups like humans." Harold was leaning forward now, resting his elbows on his knees.

Elaine didn't want to rehash the argument for them, so she placated with, "we have similar discussions, and there's no easy answer. I hate the idea of my Declan driving around with reckless humans everywhere."

"But Declan and Johnny will eventually have to interact with humans, do business with them, and study at their universities. How can they do that if we raise them in isolation here on pack lands?" Liv was obviously ready to rehash right here and now.

"Penelope is looking so grown up. I couldn't believe how much she's grown since the last time we saw her!" Elaine pivoted to change the subject to a neutral topic.

"Mmm. That one's growing up too fast for my liking." Harold shook his head and took another sip of his whiskey.

"Thank you, Elaine. Yes, Penelope is our little star. Johnny is growing ever more protective of his little sister as they both get older. I fear what will happen when she discovers boys." Liv and Elaine shared a feminine giggle.

"I hope the same for our boys. Jack is so laid back, I'm not sure he has a protective bone in his body. But Declan is growing into a strong leader, and I know he's realizing how much protection little sisters require." Theo grew pensive, staring into the fire and nudging a stray log with the toe of his boot.

"Our Penelope will not be dating anyone until her mate claims her. I've made my feelings on this subject quite clear, although my own lovely mate does not seem to take me seriously on this point." Harold made a stern face towards Liv, but her eye roll indicated she was used to it. Harry and Liv had always had a dynamic where he was too intense and stern, and she was more whimsical and carefree. Fate clearly intended for the pair to balance each other out, tempering the extremes in each personality.

"I hate the thought, but I've accepted that Theodora will probably have boyfriends before her mate claims her. Call it human influence, but I think it is probably not such a bad thing for our children to have some relationship experience before the mate bond. A successful mating takes effort." Theo looked pointedly at Elaine with that statement.

Finishing the last of her cocktail, Eliane stood. "Olivia, I'd like to go for a run. Will you join me? The moon is calling to me." She tilted her face towards the moon and extended her arms out, like an offering to Fate itself.

"I don't like the idea of my drunken mate out running alone..." Theo started to protest, but Liv interrupted him.

"She won't be alone; she'll be with me. My wolf is fierce! Just ask anybody." Liv's declaration would have landed with more force if it didn't end on a hiccup.

Harold leaned into Theo. "Let the ladies have their fun. I have guards posted at regular intervals throughout the woods as an extra security measure for your visit. And once they take off, we can give chase, eh?" Harold winked and nudged Theo's shoulder suggestively.

"I do love a good hunt, Harry." Theo looked at Elaine as he replied to Harold. Elaine shivered. She wanted some space, but she also knew a truly private moonlight run with Liv would not be possible. Their mates were simply too protective.

Liv glanced back at the house. "Let me just make sure security knows we're going so they can watch the children. C'mon, Elaine. We can undress inside."

Elaine linked her arm with her friend's as they walked to the patio door. A good moonlit run was exactly what she needed to clear her head. Her wolf always had better instincts, and maybe letting her wolf run for a while would settle her mind.

And if not, then it always felt good to give Theo a good chase.

CHAPTER 3
THEO

"Are you feeling the seventy-year itch?" Harold asked.

"The what?" Theo paused, undoing the buttons of his shirt.

"A lot of mated couples hit a rough patch around their seventieth year of being mated. It's completely normal. Matehood is an extraordinary thing, but our lives are long. Even the happiest matings have their ups and downs." Harold shrugged as he undid his own buttons.

"Did you and Olivia have a seventy-year itch?"

"Sure did. We had just gotten through the infant stage with Penelope, and we let ourselves focus a little too much on the pups. Sure, they need a lot of care and attention at that age, but you can't neglect your mate's needs. Ever." Harold punctuated his wisdom with a shift into a large silver wolf.

Theo stood there, gobsmacked. He did not know his friend had gone through that experience, and he was equally unsure if that's what was going on with his own mate. Seventy-year itch? Is that what had Elaine tied in knots? Was she...itching for something he wasn't providing her?

Theo was unsettled as he let his wolf take over. Hitting the earth with four paws, he instantly felt more grounded. His wolf always had more confidence than he did, never questioning his instincts or second guessing his decisions.

This was his favorite aspect of being a wolf shifter. When his human problems felt intractable, his wolf provided an escape.

Nose to the ground, he followed Harold to the front of the house, where his mate's scent tracked from the front door to the forest. Her trail was sweet and spicy and smelled like *home*. It called to him as much as to his wolf, who followed her scent like an arrow flying from the surest bow.

Her trail went from a straight line to a zigzag.

Left.

Then, right.

Now, along the top of a large fallen tree.

He was panting now, half from the exertion of the run and half from the thrill of the hunt. His blood pulsed through his entire body, singing for his mate. Even the forest itself came alive for him, singing its chorus of crickets to accompany the drumbeat of his heart.

She was teasing him, wanting him to give chase and not making it easy for him.

But even the gently flowing creek was not enough to keep his wolf from finding her. Tricky mate, trying to hide her scent in the water.

Harold kept pace alongside him, his wolf running nose to the ground parallel to the water. His paws pounded the sandy bank with a soft *thud* sound; his trot making an arpeggio with his footfalls. It didn't take long for them to find their mates' paw prints leaving the creek and heading up the bank.

Gotcha, little mate.

After a short distance filled with more zigs, zags, and even a couple of circles, one set of prints doubled back and one set drew him forward, beckoning him to her. His wily mate had split from her friend and was running away from them.

Harold yipped at him, signaling he was following his mate's trail back towards the house. His wolf disturbed some leaf litter on the ground as he made his pivot.

He was alone now.

It was just him and the chase.

Him and his mate.

She was running in a straight line, trying to put some distance between them. But his wolf was larger and faster.

She knew he'd overtake her easily.

He held back, forcing his muscles to slow, allowing her to run for longer and farther. His wolf needed this run as much as she did. Eventually, he closed in on his quarry.

She could never escape him. Not entirely. And not for long.

Matehood was forever.

Pouncing on her felt like coming home.

His larger black wolf's mass was too much for Elaine's sleek brown wolf to escape. They tumbled with a loud *thunk* and rolled. Theo had timed his victory to coincide with a small clearing in the forest. He righted himself first and stood directly over his mate in the moonlight. She was on her side, legs tucked. His cold, wet snout nuzzled her neck, inhaling her delicious scent. His rough tongue licked her face, savoring the taste he would never tire of sampling.

They were both panting heavily from the run. Or maybe it was the thrill of the chase.

His hackles bristled as his desire swelled. Throwing his head back, he howled his victory to the moon.

Elaine whined as she rolled her legs underneath her belly, then lifted her back legs. Her wolf presented her haunches to him, and her perfect little tail brushed his belly.

The perfect offering from his perfect mate.

Howling one more time, his wolf didn't need any instructions from him. He mounted his mate, taking advantage of their positions. He thrusted into her, coming home in the forest and the moonlight.

A cute little growl of satisfaction rumbled from her wolf as she pushed back, meeting him thrust for thrust. Her tail swished as it stiffened, then curled along her back. Theo nuzzled her neck again, bathing in her scent.

His wolf loved his mate every bit as much as he did. And his wolf adored her wolf. They were a perfect fit, her smaller body fitting perfectly underneath his taller bulk.

He growled in satisfaction when his knot took hold and claimed his mate. His pelvis crashed into her, seating his knot deep inside. He felt the swell of his knot almost painfully, and he rocked by small degrees to help ease the pressure he felt in his cock. His knot inside his mate still felt so *right*, even after all these years together. The pain was unpleasant, but it eventually sweetened into an ache that only her wolf could ease.

He sank down, making sure his weight wasn't more than her little wolf could take. He licked her face, and her wolf leaned her head back to give him better access. Her eyes squeezed closed in pleasure, and she preened under his affection.

They stayed like that for a long time, their wolves enjoying the simple pleasure of being surrounded by their mate. Life was simple and easy when it was like this. Being with your fated mate was elemental, primal.

Several minutes later, however, his knot subsided, and he slid out. A final nuzzle into his mate's neck, and they were both standing in the clearing. A cloud moved, and a moonbeam shone on his lovely mate. Her brown fur turned silver, and she looked just as beautiful as ever. The clearing was near a pond, and the sound of distant frogs croaking mixed with the smell of water and his mate's sweet scent to make an otherworldly scene.

Her wolf broke the spell with a howl, and his wolf joined her. Once both heads came down, they turned and trotted toward the house.

They took their time returning, trotting side by side at a leisurely pace. Without all the zigzags and misdirection, their journey didn't take very long. Before they broke through the tree line and entered the backyard, his wolf pushed his face into her neck.

He could feel his wolf's satisfaction. But there was a subtle undertone of worry there, too. He wanted reassurance from her wolf, but she simply shook the forest out of her fur and ran the rest of the way to the back door.

CHAPTER 4
ELAINE

The next day, everyone split into pairs. Elaine and Liv went shopping in the nearby town. Harold gave Theo a tour of recent improvements to the pack's territory. Penelope and Theodora enjoyed a playdate with Penelope's best friend, Amara. And Jack and Declan joined Johnny on a hike to the pond. The sun was bright over the vast royal property in the heart of Byrne pack territory, and it was one of the first warm days of the year, drawing people and secrets alike into the light.

Elaine and Liv walked into their third store of the afternoon, but their first jewelry store. Liv was chattering away, clearly friendly with the store's owner. But Elaine could hardly focus on the conversation; her mind was right back to the moment she found that necklace in the freezer.

Last night's run reassured her that his wolf was still loyal to her, still adored her wolf as much as ever. The warm satisfaction of reciprocated love carried her through breakfast the next morning.

She was scanning display cases for pieces in the same

collection of *that* necklace. Her vivid memory of the bold styling made it easy for her to recall details while scanning display cases for more pieces in the same set.

"We're shopping, Elaine, not conducting a warehouse inventory," Liv chided.

Elaine concluded the necklace was not purchased from this store, so she straightened next to the last display case and turned to Liv.

"I know, it's just that..." Elaine eyed the store employees. "Can we go get some coffee next?"

Liv immediately picked up on her need for a private conversation. Nodding like the queen she was, she made polite regrets with the shopkeeper and steered Elaine outside to a coffee and ice cream shop next door.

Operating on autopilot, Elaine sat where Liv instructed and tried to breathe evenly. Her stomach was roiling with the recalled anxiety of the last couple days, and her skin was clammy.

A clink snapped her out of her trance. "Drink this, it will perk you up. You look like a wilted flower, Elaine. What happened back there?" Liv pushed a latte mug towards her.

Trying to thaw her mind, she placed her stiff hands around the hot mug and inhaled the coffee aroma. Its warmth penetrated her frozen thoughts, melting her back into the present.

Liv sipped patiently, simply watching her and waiting for an explanation of what must look like odd behavior.

Might as well come out with it. If she couldn't talk to her best friend, who else could she trust? And Elaine realized at that moment that a best friend was exactly what she needed.

"I found a necklace. It was in the bottom corner of our

deep freezer. It doesn't look at all like anything I own or would pick to wear." Sniffling, a couple tears tracked down her cheeks. "I keep remembering all the times my mom's awful boyfriends betrayed or lied or cheated on her. She even found jewelry in the freezer once, too! Did I tell you that story? It happened just like it did to me right before we left to come here. She was cleaning out the fridge and found it stashed in the back of the freezer." Elaine was crying in earnest now.

"Oh, honey. I'm so sorry. No wonder you and Theo have been distant from each other since you got here. You poor thing!"

Being away from home gave her freedom to express more emotion than she would have in a shop back in Howling Forest, where curious pack members would love to eavesdrop on their queen's gossip. She clutched her coffee mug and leaned back in her chair.

"What did Theo say when you confronted him?"

"What? I didn't say anything. Just stuffed the damn thing back in the freezer and didn't say a word." Elaine wrinkled her forehead. She would not reenact the scene from her childhood. The one where her mother confronted Number Four after her discovery. "If he doesn't love me anymore or doesn't love me enough to stay loyal, I'll just leave." Elaine nodded in agreement with herself. Yes, that was the best plan. It would be hard on the children, but better than giving them front row seats to the implosion of her matehood.

"That's bullshit, Elaine. And you know it." Liv sipped her coffee with a cocked eyebrow.

"What?" Elaine said.

"I said, that's bullshit. You know Theo is your mate, given to you by Fate herself. There's no leaving your matehood. There's no falling out of love, either, for that matter." Liv punctuated her statements with a slap of her hand to the tabletop.

Elaine flinched. "I'm not sticking around if—"

"Don't lie to me, Elaine Tobin. I swear you won't like the consequences!" Liv interrupted.

"I'm not..."

"Yes, you are. You're lying to yourself and to me. You know deep down Theo still loves you. That man is every bit as loyal as my Harry is. You're letting your insecurities eat you alive. How many times over the years have we discussed your battle with insecurity? This is just another fight you need to win against the trauma of your childhood." Liv penetrated her very soul as she talked, looking directly into her eyes the whole time.

Elaine took a few sips and a few breaths to chew on her friend's words. Her finger traced the rim of her mug.

"Look, I'm giving you tough love here because I love you, Elaine. You're my best friend, and I do sympathize that finding a necklace in the freezer would be upsetting. But there's not a damn thing either of us can do about it until you talk to Theo and ask him about it." Liv softened her voice and placed a soothing hand on Elaine's wrist, giving it a little squeeze. "You know I'm here for you if that conversation doesn't go well."

Inhaling deeply, Elaine said, "I guess you're right. I was so afraid of repeating the past, I didn't give Theo a chance to explain."

"That's the spirit. Let me know how it goes after you talk to him. I expect an after-action report." Liv smiled and giggled. Her laughter was catching, and Elaine joined her.

The mood turned. Simply having a plan was a comfort to her frazzled nerves, and the friends finished their coffee and resumed strolling through the town's shopping district. Elaine felt lighter as they tried on summer dresses, and her mood was fully elevated by the time they tried on shoes. Handbags sealed the deal by putting a smile on her face.

CHAPTER 5
THEO

"I'm impressed with what you've done with the place since our last visit, Harry," Theo remarked as he put his hands in the pockets of his blue jeans. They were walking the property on a tour of recent improvements Harold and Olivia had been making as part of their economic investment plan for the pack.

"Thanks, Theo. I'm trying to make pack lands and facilities so enticing that wolves don't have any desire to leave unless absolutely necessary. My goal is for us to be as close to 100% self-contained as possible."

The men continued their stroll through an industrial area on the edge of town. The area was buzzing like a beehive of activity. Workers in high-visibility gear and hard hats drove forklifts, unloaded cargo from large trucks, and shouted orders to each other. The whirr of machinery and clunking of building materials combined into the dull roar of industry.

"This is great progress, Harry. But don't you think some interaction with humans is a good thing? If you become too isolated, their rapidly changing culture will pass you by. Before you know it, you won't know how to interact with them." Theo surveyed the bustling activity with a healthy dose of skepticism. Economic activity was something he and Elaine absolutely believed in. But they also agreed isolationism was not a sustainable policy long term, no matter how appealing the idea was on its surface.

"If something happens to Declan while he's driving among the humans, how would you feel then?" Harold asked.

"Much as I hate to admit, you can't eliminate risk in life, Harry. Are you going to avoid the other supernaturals, too? Where do you draw the line?" Theo was not trying to bait his friend into an argument. Each king had to rule his pack as he thought best. It wasn't his place to interfere with another alpha's reign.

But he also couldn't let his friend operate this way without challenging him, albeit gently.

"I don't like other supernaturals, either. Especially the witches. But other supernaturals have not come onto our pack lands in hundreds of years. The humans are right at our doorstep."

Theo pivoted and resumed their walk to keep the tension from rising too much in their conversation. He could see how entrenched his views on the topic were. It wasn't his job to convince him otherwise.

Changing the subject, Theo asked, "How is Liv doing? And the kids?"

They sidestepped a forklift carrying a pallet of bricks, then Harold answered once the beeping passed, "Johnny's doing well, about to start training as a cadet. Penelope frays my nerves with her fearlessness. I have to keep my eye on that pup constantly to see that she doesn't get into trouble. My Olivia is as lovely as ever." Harold smiled and looked at the horizon, clearly thinking of his mate with that comment.

They were now walking past the perimeter of the main industrial area, heading towards the bank of the nearby lake. As they walked, the sounds slowly faded and the smell of the water washed over them. The fresh, calm environment of the lakeshore was refreshing after walking through a hub of construction activity.

The stillness was at odds with the turmoil in his mind over Elaine's recent behavior. Maybe Harold would elaborate on his words from last night.

"Something's going on with Elaine," Theo said without preamble.

"Oh?" Harold raised his eyebrows, but they both stood facing the water.

"I would do anything for my mate. I would provide her anything she needs. Literally *anything*. But it frustrates the fuck out of me when I don't know what she needs." Theo had more pent up frustration than he realized, apparently.

"You asked her?"

"Of course I did. That was the first thing I did. But she wouldn't give me anything. Just clammed up." Theo exhaled deeply.

"Wolves are lucky to have long lives, and the blessing of a mate allows us to live untold centuries. But forever is a long time. You have to keep nourishing the matehood to maintain it. My guess? Nothing is broken. Elaine just needs a little romance." Harold shrugged like that was the most natural and intuitive conclusion possible.

The bastard.

But maybe he was right.

"Romance? That's your advice?" Theo asked.

"Yes." Harold nodded. "Look, I get it. You and me? We're like the sandy beach here along the water's edge. We are smooth and constant. But our mates? Those two are like the water. They aren't still, and their waves are as much a part of who they are as the wetness is a part of the water." Harold bent down to pick up a palm-sized rock. "If the water gets too still, you gotta throw a rock in it and make some waves." Harold threw the rock like a shot-put into the lake. It made a satisfying splash, and soon the waves were lapping at the sand by their feet.

"Romance?"

"Romance."

After a moment's reflection, Theo grabbed his phone out of his pocket and started texting.

THEO

Hey, Killian. Are you available to watch the kids for a week? I'd feel better if a soldier stayed at the house.

KILLIAN

Yes, sir.

THEO

Good.

Theo looked out at the water. He needed to make waves.

THEO

Don't tell anyone. I'm planning a surprise for the Queen. I'll tell the kids right before we leave.

KILLIAN

Copy that, sir.

Theo nodded to Harold. He would try romance. He could throw rocks if that's what it took to make his beloved Elaine happy.

CHAPTER 6
ELAINE

"Did you girls have a fun day today?" Elaine asked as she tucked Theodora into bed.

"We did, mama! Didn't we, Penny?" Theodora looked at her friend lying in the bed beside her.

"It was fun watching the boys," Penelope giggled. It wasn't long before Theodora joined her, and Elaine was dealing with a pair of silly girls nowhere near ready to fall asleep. But royal visits were not frequent, and she loved to see her daughter having fun with her friend. Her own childhood had been overshadowed by the heavy burden of grown-up worries, even when she was as young as Theodora. Her daughter was happy and carefree in the way all little girls deserved to be.

"Now, what's this I hear about boy-watching?" Liv joined them on the bed.

"We found the boys playing on the tire swing at the pond, and we climbed into a tree to watch them. I think Amara is in love with Johnny," Penelope stated with authority.

"Yeah, and you're in love with Jack!" Theodora pounced on her friend and began tickling her.

"Girls, girls - you have to calm down or you'll never fall asleep," Elaine tried, and failed, to simmer down the pair's antics.

Each mother snuggled her daughter in a ploy to disentangle the girls. The strategy worked, and eventually Elaine and Liv could leave the bedroom.

"You know they're not likely to get any sleep tonight. They were faking it when we left them," Liv said as they walked down the hall.

"I know. But let them have their fun. We have a very early flight home in the morning, and letting her sleep through it isn't a bad strategy." Elaine shrugged.

They parted ways and said their goodnights at the end of the hall, where the two women split off to their respective mates. Their evening had been relaxed, with each pair eating on their own time and spending as much time visiting as possible.

The boys were out all day, apparently swimming in the pond with surreptitious spectators in a nearby tree.

Theo and Harold visited a local bar before returning to the house later that evening, where Elaine and Liv were enjoying the sunset (and wine) on the patio. A relaxing day all around, and Elaine felt lighter having shared her worries with her best friend and planning to discuss the necklace with Theo when they returned home.

BACK HOME FROM their visit to Byrne pack, Elaine decided there was no time like the present. She fed the children dinner and let them relax with a movie in the living room.

Theo was catching up on work in his home office, where Elaine joined him.

Closing the door, she turned and said, "Theo, we need to talk."

"Hmm?" Theo responded without looking up from the report he was reading.

Elaine slowly dropped the diamond necklace onto the desk, directly in his line of sight.

Theo froze.

"What the hell is this, Elaine?" He held the necklace, but looked directly at Elaine.

She had his full attention now. Good.

"I'm here to ask you the same thing, Theo." Elaine crossed her arms.

"Is this what has been bothering you lately?" Theo asked.

"Answer my question! Who is that necklace for? Who is she!" Elaine was now leaning over his desk, jabbing her finger at the offensive jewelry.

Her strategy for this conversation flew right out the window.

O'well. In for a penny, in for a pound. She aimed to get the truth out of him. Might as well get right to it. At least she wasn't crying. She didn't want to become her mother, sobbing over betrayal.

"Who is—" Theo shook his head like a cartoon character. He dropped the necklace on his desktop and ran both hands through his hair while blowing a long breath out. "That necklace is for you, *mate*. Of course it is for you. It would never be for anybody else. How could you even think that?" He walked around his desk and gently held her shoulders. "How could you possibly ask me that, Elaine?"

Two things happened at once: her anger deflated, and she flinched at the flash of hurt on his face. But, to be fair...

"Then why on earth was it hidden in the corner of the deep freeze, Theo? You know I'm the one who puts food in there most of the time."

"Because, mate, I bought it as our mating anniversary gift. But since our anniversary is still five weeks away, I couldn't think of anywhere else to hide it that the kids wouldn't find. You remember that year they found your earrings I kept in my desk drawer?"

He was right. The boys found his desk key and got the idea to snoop in his office. Their victory at finding a pair of emerald earrings was short-lived once Theo discovered what had happened. The poor pups couldn't sit for a week.

"So you planned ahead for my anniversary gift and hid it in the freezer so the kids wouldn't find it?" As Elaine spoke, she realized it sounded exactly like something Theo would do.

"Mmhmm."

"Well, then. I'm sorry Theo." She bit her lower lip. "But that hiding place was a terrible idea."

"You're forgiven, mate." Theo paused and rubbed the back of his neck in thought. "You're also right. That hiding place wasn't a good idea. I assumed you'd never notice a small addition at the bottom since you keep things so organized in there. At least not for the couple of weeks I needed to hide it."

"Worst fucking assumption, Theo," Elaine said. How can men be so smart and so dumb at the same time?

"Tell me, mate, why did you immediately think the worst? Have I given you any cause to think I would...what? Buy another woman jewelry and hide it in your house?"

Theo's face scrunched in confusion. When he put it like that...it didn't sound good.

She gulped.

"I dunno. Our life is so routine these days. So predictable, so regular. I guess I saw a necklace that looked so striking, so bold and different from anything I would wear. I thought maybe you decided to exchange this bran muffin for a spicy chili pepper." Gesturing to herself, she tried to shrug and look at her feet, but Theo wouldn't let her. His one large hand kept her shoulder in place while his other hand lifted her chin to force eye contact.

"Bran muffin?" Theo tilted his head like a curious puppy.

His small, quiet office suddenly became a sarcophagus for her pride.

"You know what I mean." Elaine waved off his reaction.

Theo grew serious and continued, "I'm going to say this once, mate. I hope to Fate it is the last time you need to hear it. You are not your mother." He placed a hand on each cheek and cradled her face. "The death of your father destroyed her. As it would for any surviving mate. But she held on long enough to raise you and see you safely settled with me. And for that, I will always respect her and be grateful to her.

"But she was a broken woman, and you are nothing like her. And I would never treat you like those bastards she took up with after your father died." Theo's finger tenderly traced the outline of his claiming mark, raising goosebumps in its wake.

Even after all these years since he first claimed her, the outline of his bite mark where her shoulder met her neck was still visible for all to see. And sensitive as hell.

Elaine simply stood in his arms, staring into his eyes.

His words washed over her and a shiver ran down her spine. A small opening in her heart tenderly closed, like a wound finally healing. There would always be a scar to mark the event, but it was no longer an open vulnerability.

Stroking her cheek with his thumb, Theo let his words sink in for a moment before he released her. Turning to lock the office door, he spoke to her over his shoulder.

"Now, put that necklace on and take off all your clothes."

CHAPTER 7
ELAINE

"W-w-what? Theo, the chil—"

"The children are watching a movie on the other side of the house. I just locked the door. Now, strip little mate." Theo slowly advanced on her while methodically unbuckling his belt. "And put on that necklace."

Elaine knew that voice. And that look. Resistance was futile when he went into king mode like that. She began removing her pants.

But her impatient mate was already naked by the time she stood back up.

"You have three seconds to become naked, or I'm going to tear that shirt right off your perfect body. One..." Theo was stalking her now. She instinctively took a step backwards.

"Two."

She was too flustered to get the damn shirt off. Dropping her shaking arms to her side, she huffed, "Oh just do it already. I'll never make it before thr—"

A loud ripping sound filled the office as Theo didn't

hesitate to grab her t-shirt and rip it down the front. Her sports bra was next. The poor thing didn't stand a chance against Theo's strength and lust.

Both naked, Theo slowly picked up the necklace and dangled it in front of her. "Turn."

She gathered her hair off her neck as she followed his command. The metal still had some chill from its time in the freezer, and it contrasted with the heat coming off her claiming bite. Her nipples went turgid immediately.

Wordlessly, he placed his hands on her shoulders and angled her in front of his desk. Then he swept his arm across the surface to clear it in dramatic fashion. Elaine's eyes widened as important pack business papers and file folders fluttered to the ground. The pencil holder clattered as it hit the hardwood floor.

The last pen stopped rolling and the office items all settled quietly. Her heavy breathing was the only sound. Theo slowly pushed her shoulders so she was bent face down over his now empty desk. The pendant *clunked* as it landed on the office desk's surface.

His mouth was at her ear, and his fingers were inside her pussy. "Do you know why I selected that necklace for you?" His fingers slowly slid in and out of her as he licked her claiming mark. As he waited for her reply, he rotated his wrist so a second finger could join as he rubbed her G-spot.

She moaned and spread her legs wider, thankful for the traction of the plush rug.

"I wanted you to wear something as bold and strikingly beautiful as you are. All your other pieces are so demure, so sweet, so regal." His fingers were pumping in earnest now, working her G-spot with practiced precision. "But I saw that necklace in the shop, and I thought it captured your strength and your bravery. I wanted you to wear a necklace that matched your spirit, not your other jewels."

She arched her back and cried out as an orgasm ripped through her. She slapped her hands on the surface of the desk as her feet lifted to tippy toes. The diamond scraped against the wooden surface, the weight a reminder of how she got into this position. Her body was crying out for Theo to take her hips and slam home.

And that's exactly what he did.

His thrusts extended her orgasm, and she had no rest before the next climax started building. Theo bent his knees for leverage, then lifted her hips with his cock so her feet no longer touched the rug. Her legs went limp as his grip on her hips and the thrusts of his cock suspended her, body and mind.

Her blood was singing for him, and her mind was flying. Without the weight of her body to steady them, her legs trembled and twitched almost violently. She extended her arms to grip the opposite edge of the desk.

Theo pounded into her. Steady, even, relentless strokes. His exertion had him growling low and deep.

"I want you to wear that necklace, mate. And I want you to think of this conversation every time you do. I want you to touch that diamond and remember how hard you make my cock. I want you — *hnnng*!"

Theo couldn't finish his words because his body was finishing inside her. Elaine's insides filled with his warmth as his body shook with release. He still suspended her hips with his grip, and she had no choice but to follow him over the edge.

For a long moment, they were nothing more than a connected mass of shaking, blissed out bodies.

Slowly, he lowered her hips, and he lowered his torso

over her back. Still inside her, he placed his hands over hers on the table. He sucked on her claiming mark.

"I love you, Elaine. My mate. Don't you ever doubt my love again." He kissed her cheek then rested his own on top. They shared breaths like that until they finally came back to Earth.

Once they were standing, Elaine turned to face him. The necklace was warm now, heated by her body and their passion as it hung between the tops of her breasts. "I love you, too. You're my mate, and I promise to keep my insecurities from making me forget how much you love me." She pulled his head down to seal her promise with a slow, luxurious kiss. "Just...please try to remember not all of us had an idyllic childhood, growing up as a royal prince with two loving parents."

"Yes, I was blessed with a wonderful childhood. That is true. But you are now blessed with a wonderful matehood." Theo winked at her. "We can enjoy giving our pups the childhood everyone deserves. All I want is for you to remember how much I love you, and for you to let yourself be happy that you are now living the life you should have always had." He fingered the chain of rubies suspending the pendant, and the gentle touch contrasted with the force of his words.

Elaine wrapped her arms around her mate, letting his words soak in. They stood, basking in the afterglow, simply cherishing each other before Theo spoke again.

"Oh, and little mate?" He kissed her neck, nosing her hair out of the way before whispering in her ear, "I think bran muffins are *delicious*."

CHAPTER 8
THEO

A week later, Theo was running late to the ribbon cutting. Theodora was a whirlwind, and he honestly wasn't sure if she was ready or not. Declan was ready on time, but Jack couldn't find a pair of matching shoes to save his life. He was on the verge of telling him to shift and attend the ceremony in his wolf form when his phone chirped.

KILLIAN

Ready, sir.

THEO

Excellent. We are running late, but I will get us there before her speech ends.

KILLIAN

See you soon.

THEO

Thanks. See you soon.

"All right kids, let's load up and head out. Your mother will be speaking soon." Theo wrangled the trio into the car, which, for some reason, was more difficult than mobilizing an entire squadron of brand new cadets.

As he drove, Theo said, "All right, tell me who's excited for summer vacation? School's almost out."

"I am, daddy!" Theodora said.

"That's great, sweetheart!" Theo looked at her in the rearview mirror.

"And I bet Penny is excited to see Jack again," she giggled.

"Shut up, what are you even talking about?" Jack grumped at her.

"Watch your tone when speaking with your little sister, Jack," Theo's stern voice elicited a prompt apology from Jack.

Theodora stuck her tongue out.

Declan helpfully changed the subject. "I can't wait to get my driver's license this summer. Killian said he'd let me practice in his Jeep in the training fields."

"That's great, Declan. The best way to become a safe driver is lots of practice." Theo was met with an eye roll, but the boys knew better than to sass him too much.

"Speaking of Killian, I want all you kids to listen up." Theo paused to make sure he had everyone's attention. "I'm going to take your mother on a vacation, and Killian is going to stay with you while we're gone."

"What vacation?"

"Where are you going?"

"Can I come, too?"

Theo laughed at the simultaneous questions. He raised his hand to quell the interrogation. "We'll only be gone for a week. I planned this as a surprise, and your mother has no idea. I'm doing it to give your mother a little romance, to give us some adult time. We are going to an island in the

Caribbean where I've rented a bungalow on a private beach."

"But why?" Declan asked in confusion.

"Because I've recently been reminded that meeting the needs of my mate includes giving her the excitement and spontaneity she craves," Theo explained.

"Are we boring, daddy?" Theodora asked.

"No, sweetheart. She loves us, and we are all very important to her. But mama also needs some special attention just from daddy sometimes. I don't always remember that, but I'm going to fix that now," Theo explained to his youngest.

"Whatever, at least Killian is going to stay with us. Maybe he'll teach me some new wrestling moves," Jack said. "At least if y'all are going to be all gross and lovey-dovey, it'll be on an island far away."

They continued to discuss the upcoming week and plans for this summer's school vacation until Theo pulled into a spot in the town hall parking lot. Theo carried Theodora on his shoulders while Declan and Jack walked alongside them.

After a few minutes of walking, they heard the dull roar of a large crowd. The pack assembled in front of a building standing just past the end of downtown. It was surrounded by the forest that gave the town its name, but the downtown sidewalks connected the building to the town.

The street in front was closed for the event, allowing the pack to have a block party. The sounds of merry wolves rose as Theo and his family approached. A vendor was handing out free cotton candy to enthusiastic children. The scent of sizzling meat wafted over them from an unseen grill.

"Ooh, I want some cotton candy!" Theodora wiggled on

Theo's shoulders, and he lifted her down so she could make a beeline for the cotton candy cart. She quickly paired off with a couple of girls her age to enjoy the treat.

"Before you boys take off, I want you both to know I expect you to watch over your sister while we're gone. Killian will stay at the house and watch over the three of you, but I want you two to keep a special eye on Theodora."

Theo looked each teenager in the eye, infusing his words with royal command. He wasn't worried about Killian's ability to hold down the fort for a week, but he wanted his sons to learn responsibility and the importance of looking out for each other.

His pack would keep them safe, but one day they would have mates to watch over and protect, and that was a trickier proposition. Best to let them practice with an easier assignment.

"Yes, sir," they said in unison.

"Killian!" Declan waved to the approaching soldier.

"Perfect timing. Theodora is over there, eating too much cotton candy with her friends." Theo pointed out his daughter. "Any questions, don't hesitate to text me."

"Understood, sir." Killian nodded at Theo, then turned to Declan and Jack. "Y'all make it to the meat cart yet?" When they both shook their head, Killian started walking.

Smiling, Theo wormed his way through the crowd to the front row. An easy task, as everyone parted for the king. He looked up at his stunning wife, standing behind a large red ribbon tied between two Greek columns. She stood under the building's tall front porch, at the top of a flight of concrete steps.

Behind her, a large banner read, *Tobin Library & Archives Grand Reopening.* Elaine held comically large scissors. Flanking her were the pack archivist and the preservation architect who led the work to restore the library and archives building.

Elaine took a confident step forward, and the crowd instantly hushed. She didn't have to command them; her regal presence as their beloved queen was enough to capture their attention. And also their adoration, he noted with satisfaction.

"Thank you all for coming to our grand reopening ceremony," Elaine began.

Theo waited patiently for her roving eyes to connect with him in the crowd. He knew the moment she found him because her delicate hand lifted, and she stroked the diamond pendant hanging from her new necklace.

The gesture went straight to his cock.

He had insisted she wear the necklace today because he wanted her to wear it when he whisked her away right after her speech. Theo didn't anticipate the effect it would have on him; he could barely even listen to what she was saying.

"...and after two years of hard work restoring the building, I am pleased to announce..." Elaine was talking, but his ears were pounding with desire for his lovely little mate.

"...Library and Archives is the best of all the North American packs..."

Theo subtly adjusted his pants. How would he survive until he had her alone? A trickle of sweat ran down his temple.

"...by cutting this ribbon, I now declare..."

Theo couldn't wait any longer. He saw the large scissors snip the red ribbon, and the crowd erupted in applause. He used the sound to mask a moan as Elaine handed over the scissors and gave the audience a beautiful smile.

Theo broke from the crowd and stalked up the steps.

"Theo? What are you—" Elaine's words were cut off

when he scooped her up, bridal style. She shrieked and instinctively wrapped her arms around his neck.

"Members of the Tobin pack!" Theo's voice boomed and the raucous whistles, playful catcalls, and claps died down.

"Y'all have been blessed for many years now to have Elaine as your beautiful, capable, kind Queen." Theo's declaration elicited whoops of approval from the crowd, including a couple people calling out, *long live the Queen!*

Theo squeezed her against his chest as Elaine squirmed in his arms. Her body radiated heat. He continued, "Today, she presided over the grand reopening of this jewel of the Tobin pack, our restored Library and Archives. But now, I must take my jewel away for a short time. For she is not only your beloved queen, but she is also my mate." Theo waggled his eyebrows playfully, and the crowd went wild.

Whistles, *atta boys*, and howls rang out in response.

Elaine buried her head in his neck, and he heard a moan escape her.

Theo carried her down the steps, and the crowd parted down the middle for them. He walked with his mate in his arms through their pack, surrounded by the pack's love and devotion for their queen. *His* queen.

Her thumb rubbed up and down his neck as Elaine clung to him while they made their exit.

Killian had assembled the kids at the back of the crowd. Theo set down their mother so they could hug her.

"We'll miss you, mama!" Theodora bear hugged Elaine's legs.

"Why is that, sweetheart?" Elaine looked at Theo to resolve her confusion, but it was Declan who answered her.

"Dad's taking you to some private island for a week. Sounds boring if you ask me, but I hope you have fun." Declan hugged his mother next.

"What?" Elaine gasped. "I can't leave you kids just like that! Theo..."

Killian interrupted Elaine's protests. "I'll be staying with the kids, ma'am. Don't you worry about a thing. I'll take good care of them while y'all are gone." Killian nodded as he spoke, confident he could handle his mission.

"Bye, mom," Jack came in for a hug next.

Elaine sniffed and wiped away a tear. She buried her face in Jack's shaggy hair and swayed slightly with him in her arms.

"We'll be fine, mom. It is just a week." Jack awkwardly patted her shoulder, and that's when Theo intervened.

"All right, that's enough. I've given Killian all the instructions he needs, the fridge is stocked with plenty of food for the week, and we have a flight to catch. If there are any questions, they can call or text."

"But..." Elaine's face was red, and she was losing the battle against her tears. Theo took her hand, interlacing their fingers. Pulling her away from the circle of children, he tucked her next to him and gave her a slow kiss on her fore-head. "It's time for us to go, mate. We'll see you kids in a week."

He began walking to the rookie deputy who would drive them to the airport. Their bags were already loaded. He had to keep tugging on Elaine to maintain her progress; she kept looking back and waving at the kids.

Eventually, she accepted her fate, and they were on their way to the airport. Elaine nestled into his side, and he could feel the moment her resistance melted.

He leaned down and kissed her claiming mark before whispering into her ear, "I love you, Elaine. You're my trea-sure. I can't wait until the only thing you're wearing is that necklace."

The End

Thank you for reading Theo and Elaine's story! Turn the page for a sample of Declan's love story, Searching for Sabine.

For the latest news in Howling Forest, please join my newsletter at www.bethdeweese.com/newsletter.

SEARCHING FOR SABINE

CHAPTER 1

Declan Tobin dreaded his twenty-fifth birthday.

Which is why he went all out with his birthday party. It was the last time he'd be able to truly cut loose before Tuesday, his actual birthday. He sipped his whiskey and surveyed the scene, which was a damn good party, he thought.

Of course, the crown prince of the Tobin pack turning twenty-five was sure to draw a large crowd from friends, family, and surrounding wolf packs. But that didn't diminish the fact that he needed a distraction, and this party was doing its job.

The night air had the perfect amount of chill to make the large bonfire an attractive option, but not so much bite that the groups enjoying the open bar or the buffet were cold. Which meant that the women didn't need heavy coats covering their dresses.

In the middle of the large converted barn turned event venue on his parents' property, a mix of couples were swaying to the band's slow number. His mother snuggled into his dad's chest as the king danced with his beloved queen. Declan tipped up his glass to polish off the last of his drink when a hand clapped on his shoulder.

"You ready, old man?"

Declan growled. "This old man is perfectly capable of kicking his baby brother's ass, and don't you forget it."

"Oh, come on now, what kind of a younger brother would I be if I didn't ask how you're feeling," Jack asked while tipping his glass up to request the bartender for a refill. "And you know Theodora is the baby of the family, so don't even start."

Declan decided to get this conversation out of the way, otherwise his younger brother would hound him all night. He wanted tonight to be a diversion, not a reminder.

Jack could be tenacious, and Declan was in no mood for it. He signaled the bartender for another whiskey before the brothers sauntered to the back corner of the barn. With the large doors open on both ends, partygoers could wander all around the backyard property.

Clutching his glass, Declan resumed their conversation. "I keep thinking I didn't make the most of my time before now. And now it's basically over. This party is the last bit of fun I'll get to have before Tuesday. It doesn't feel like enough." Declan took a long sip and let the burn distract from the anxiety tightening in his chest.

"Yeah, but isn't the ability to scent your mate something to look forward to? You'll finally get to search for your woman. Aren't you glad the anticipation will finally end?" Jack was twenty-three and curious about matehood. He always had been, even as kids.

Growing up, Jack's attitude toward matehood was in the middle of his older friend Killian, who was desperate for his mate and couldn't wait to turn twenty-five, and himself, who dreaded the whole idea of Fate determining the one person he had to spend forever with.

"You don't get it, do you? You never have. My choices are about to go *poof*." The band's next song was an upbeat dance number, and Declan's resolve lifted with the music. "But I plan to make the most of tonight. I suggest you do the same thing. You have barely two good years left before it's your turn."

As the slow-dancing couples were replaced by more energetic types, Declan saw his dad escorting his mom off the dance floor. He whispered something in her ear while he fingered her necklace, a large diamond pendant with small rubies along the chain. His mom blushed instantly as she clutched his hand. Her eyes caught Declan and Jack standing together, and she steered them over to their corner.

"We're having a great time, honey. I hope you're enjoying your party as much as I am," the queen asked her son.

"I am. Thanks again for helping organize such a great event, Mom. I appreciate you." Declan leaned in and kissed her cheek. She beamed back at him, basking in his praise and gratitude.

"Well, I think it is time for the old folks to head home. Leave you young wolves to your fun. Isn't that right, Elaine?" The king smirked in a way that said there was nothing odd about his intentions for the rest of their evening.

Turning serious, the king looked directly at his sons. "Don't do anything you'll regret tonight. Finding your mate is the best thing that will ever happen to you. Don't make a decision you'll regret after meeting her." He squeezed his mate around the shoulders to emphasize his point.

Jack gulped, and Declan nodded. Both men mumbled a "yes sir".

"Let's go, Theo," his mom whispered. She touched the diamond pendant around her neck as she spoke. "Good night, boys. I love you."

"Love you too, Mom," Jack and Declan said in chorus. Elaine reached out and squeezed Declan's forearm as Theo walked them through the wide barn doors.

Chuckling, Jack watched them walk back to the royal residence, Elaine tucked under Theo's arm. "See? Mom and dad seem happy. Looks like matehood suits them."

"They were lucky, Jack. Not every mated pair is that lucky. Or that disgustingly happy. Plus, dad is always so structured and regimented. Of course, he likes the idea of a single mate selected for him by fate. It suits his personality."

Declan abandoned Jack and headed toward the bonfire. He didn't want to discuss the topic any further, especially not when he was hankering for a little variety. The warmth from the large flames attracted several groups of women seeking relief from the chill, and Declan savored the fact he still had options. He slowed his walk while he considered which one he wanted to choose for the evening.

Several clusters included women from his own pack. Not a bad way to go, but he already had history with each of them, and there was a chance they wouldn't be interested in revisiting a final fling with their prince before his twenty-fifth. At least not without persuasion.

Scanning faces in the firelight, he decided his chance of success would be highest with someone unfamiliar, here to party and mingle with someone new. When faced with multiple options, Declan always preferred the path of least resistance.

He settled on a trio of women from another pack. Inviting neighboring packs was a smart move. Variety was the spice of life, after all.

"You ladies having a good time at the party?" Declan deployed his best come-fuck-me smile.

"Hey, it's the birthday boy! Cheers!" One blonde greeted him with tipsy enthusiasm, and the other two women followed suit. They all raised their cocktails to him and cheered enthusiastically.

"Such a great party, Declan. But a human band? That was unexpected." The brunette hiccupped.

"Yeah, I had to pay them extra to come in from Nashville, but I thought they were worth it. I also paid them extra to be completely gone before it's time for the pack run."

"You're so smart," the other blonde observed, the alcohol giving her speech a sibilant quality.

Outwardly, Declan smiled at the women. But internally, he cringed. They were all too drunk to really give consent, and he had no interest in a sloppy quickie. As he surveyed the trio, he realized they held no real attraction for him.

"Enjoy the party ladies. I need to make the rounds. Be a good host and all." He raised his glass and tried not to gloat at their pouting. It was still nice to be appreciated.

Declan floated from one conversation to another as he circumvented the bonfire. Eventually, he drifted towards the food table and snagged a meat skewer or three. He enjoyed a little protein before a run.

While he chewed, he looked up at the full moon. What would it feel like to have a mate? Would it chafe to be accountable to another person? What if they didn't enjoy being around each other? What if he didn't like her family;

would he be forced to spend time with people he didn't like?

Declan stretched his shoulders between bites. He heard a little pop as one of his seams busted a stitch. The bulk he was putting on as he approached twenty-five was coming in too quickly for him to keep up with new clothes.

He sighed at the reminder of impending change. Maybe he should get his hair cut, too. Running his fingers through his thick, shoulder-length hair, he contemplated getting a crew cut. It wouldn't matter anymore that wolf females loved a good man-bun; a crew cut would be so much easier to maintain.

"You're moping," a deep voice said from behind.

Pulled from his thoughts, Declan turned and smiled at the Tobin pack sheriff. "You're supposed to be off duty, Sheriff Sullivan."

"I'm wearing jeans and a flannel shirt, same as you, prince Declan." Connor emphasized his point by swirling his bottle of beer. "But I'm never off duty from keeping you in line. You sure threw a good party tonight. Why aren't you happier about it?"

"I am. I'm just thinking about everything that's about to change. The uncertainty—it has me unsettled, I guess." Declan shrugged and returned his gaze to the full moon.

"Mmm. That's reasonable, I suppose." Connor took a drink of his beer and joined Declan in admiring the full moon. "I can still remember what it felt like to be on the cusp of my twenty-fifth birthday. I was so full of hope back then. And excitement. Felt like I was about to embark on a grand adventure."

The pack's beloved sheriff still hadn't found his mate. And without the magic of the mate bond, he aged on a human time scale. Connor was mid-forties with salt and pepper hair framing laugh lines around his eyes. Even his skinned tanned more easily, so his complexion was darker than the typical pack member. Oh, he was still fit as a fiddle and enjoyed the muscles that bulk up when shifter males reach maturity at twenty-five. But he continued to age without his mate.

"I'm sorry, Connor. I don't mean to complain to you of all people—" Declan was interrupted by Connor's raised hand. The sheriff was proud and didn't tolerate anyone's pity.

"I'm not here to give you a hard time, Declan. I sought you out to say the band is playing their last song. I'll see that they clear out, then we can shift and run."

Declan nodded. "Thanks, Sheriff." His wolf stretched and yawned inside him. Declan might be feeling a little restless at the party, but his wolf was utterly bored. He had been sleeping a majority of the time lately, uninterested in Declan's attempts to enjoy his last days of freedom. But the thought of a large pack run under a full moon was rousing him.

Everyone maintained their current mixing and mingling while the human band packed up their gear. To their eyes, nothing about the party had changed. But Declan, and his wolf, could sense the shift, the excitement for a large pack run. It was common to run with wolves in your own pack, but multiple packs running together was a special occasion.

Finally, Declan saw Connor double checking all humans were gone. With a final sniff of the air to confirm, Connor nodded the all-clear.

Declan climbed onto a table and clapped his hands.

"Thank you for coming, everybody!" He paused as the crowd assembled around him and quieted. "It's been a great party, and I appreciate everyone who traveled to attend. Now, we're going to take a run under the full moon."

Whoops and howls greeted his announcement. "We will head south, and once we leave the royal residence's property, we'll have a hundred and twenty-five acres of pack land to run through. It's beautiful land, and I'm excited to share it with our guests." Lifting his whiskey glass to the crowd, he continued, "Here's to making the best of mated life! Cheers!"

Half the crowd returned his cheers, but half were already undressing. The party became a mix of half-dressed and fully naked people, and several wolves. Declan dismounted his impromptu podium and quickly undressed before he shifted.

The large gathering of wolves howled at the moon in unison. Some wolves nuzzled a neighbor, while others ran around sniffing the newcomers. Declan's wolf preened at the sight. He loved seeing so many wolves all in one place.

As his wolf took position in the lead, Declan couldn't help but let his mood be buoyed by his wolf's happiness. One of the best parts of being a wolf shifter was the ability to lay down your worries and just let your wolf run for a while.

Declan's wolf led the assembly out of the barn and towards the tree line south of the main house, and he felt the tension uncoil around his chest. For the first time in a while, he could truly breathe.

As the smells of the barn, the party's food, and human musicians faded, Declan's tension faded, too.

Inhaling deeply, he took in the smell of the forest, the scent of every prey animal that crossed this way in the last day, the freshness of the soil being churned up by their paws. Even the scent of exertion from the wolves on the run added to the milieu that set Declan and his wolf free. Even if only a temporary reprieve, it was exactly what he needed.

As his wolf panted with the increasing exertion of the run, Declan let his anxiety over his upcoming birthday melt. Not entirely. He still dreaded the idea of being forced to mate with someone he didn't choose.

His wolf, however, was confident it would all be okay. No matter what happened after Tuesday, his wolf was confident it would be all okay, that he would find a way to enjoy his life. And that gave Declan comfort.

The pack weaved through the forest, following Declan's lead while fanning out to give each wolf room to run. Each wolf had its own personality when it came to the run; some preferred to leap over fallen logs and large branches, some preferred to dodge around obstacles.

The pounding of multiple sets of paws on the ground created a magical air to the evening. The moonlight glinted off various shades of fur, but the many different bodies coalesced into a single pack entity, running in unison and creating a unique energy.

It was better than any drug the humans could create. There was nothing in the entire world that compared to the synchronicity of a pack run.

He led them across a small creek, and the splashing of the water created an echo in the forest. His blood was pumping strongly now, rushing through every vein and pulse point. It magnified the rhythm of his heart. He had no thoughts but the run.

Setting the pace.

Keeping the pack together.

Challenging them to run faster, matching his every turn and pivot.

His muscles burned and melted away his fear and worry and anxiety. The heat from his exertion burned away the tension over his upcoming birthday.

Hours passed, and the pack achieved flow. Unity. They ran as one. Wolves had incredible stamina, so the run was still going strong when daylight began to peek over the treetops.

Eventually, Declan returned them to the barn. The party was already cleaned up and some meat kebabs and bottles of water set out for a post-run protein snack.

The sweaty, panting mass of naked bodies scattered to recover clothing and grab food. Everyone, including Declan, was relaxed and peaceful. Wolf shifters felt euphoria from post-run endorphins similar to humans. Like most aspects of wolf shifter physiology, the effect was stronger than the human equivalent.

Even the grilled meat kebabs tasted more savory than usual. For a while, no one spoke; they simply ate and cooled off and enjoyed the larger than average size of the pack run. Larger runs resulted in greater feelings of contentment and satisfaction than a typical run, and Declan didn't want to interrupt the mood.

He walked through the mass of shifters, silently assessing everyone's condition. A few times he put a bottle of water into the hand of a shifter looking a little too dehydrated. He noticed one of the smaller females from another pack wasn't eating. Smaller wolves needed post-run protein even more than the larger wolves, so he grabbed a plate and piled a couple kebabs on it to hand her. He inspected an elbow with a scratch, but determined it would heal too quickly to justify bringing out the first-aid kit.

Once satisfied everyone was recovering well, Declan slumped into one of the chairs he positioned toward the horizon. He felt invigorated and relaxed, ready to watch the sunrise. Ready for whatever Fate had planned for him.

CHAPTER 2

Declan felt miserable as he stared at his computer screen. Mondays were never his favorite, but this morning he was extra grumpy about it. Try as he might, this report was not holding his attention.

Declan worked at Ainran Policy Group to gain experience assimilating into human society. He'd be resigning soon, another consequence of turning twenty-five.

It would not be soon enough. His office chair was uncomfortable, the computer desk was not at the right height anymore, and he needed to loosen his belt, again.

He had heard about the bulking that naturally occurs as a wolf shifter male approaches his twenty-fifth birthday. But no one talked about the restlessness. His inner wolf was pacing, pushing against him to bust out and run free. He felt itchy from the inside out.

His wolf was never chaotic like this. They were in sync at least, but he would prefer if their synchronicity wasn't over a mix of anticipation and agitation.

Running his fingertips over his scalp, he again contemplated if he would cut his hair short. His bun was too tight this morning.

Even the florescent lights in the human office made his eyes wince. Huffing out his annoyance, Declan grabbed his coffee mug and headed to the break room. A little pop sounded as another stitch gave way somewhere. He really needed to buy some new clothes.

Declan enjoyed working for the human research organization. It served pack interests for him to become knowledgeable in human government public policies and regulations. On a personal level, he enjoyed learning more about the quirks and personalities of his human coworkers, the thousand little customs that made humans delightfully unique.

None of them knew about the existence of supernatural beings or about his wolf, of course, but the policy wonks who worked here were generally kind, thoughtful, and intelligent.

He rounded the corner of a row of tan cubicles and saw a group decorating the break room with string lights. Declan leaned against the doorframe to observe the merry band of coworkers. His boss, Emily, stood on a step stool, arms extended and draped with Christmas lights. Her back was to him as she glowed with the little white lights across her arms and shoulders and even through her blonde hair.

She looks like some sort of angel, Declan thought.

A moment later, it dawned on him that he should probably offer his six-foot-two body to help hang the lights. Humans were so frightfully fragile, and none of them should be standing on a step stool, much less a delicate female wearing a pencil skirt and heels.

"Isn't it a little early for holiday decorations?" Declan greeted the group with a chuckle. "It's barely fall yet. Can't we at least make it past Halloween before hanging the Christmas lights?"

Emily looked at him over her shoulder. "We're early this year so the decorations can do double duty with James' retirement party."

Declan stood next to her, the step stool making her height equal to his. Declan gently extricated the sting lights from her arms and shoulders and used his much longer arms to lift them.

"Thank you, Decs. When I hired you, I had no idea how handy your massive frame would be," Emily laughed as she dismounted and joined Amy at the box of decorations.

Declan continued to hang the rest of the string along the top of the standard break room bulletin board, over the cabinets above the sink, and around the doorframe. He enjoyed the chatter of Amy and Emily deciding which decorations were the most neutral and thus appropriate for the retirement party. Another coworker was hanging party signs on the walls.

I'll miss these cheerful humans, Declan mused. Once he turned twenty-five, he'd have to resign his job at the human organization to focus on helping his parents run the pack.

And to focus on the search for his mate.

The dread gripping his chest returned. He couldn't get a full breath, and he gave undue attention to securing the end of the string of lights to give him a moment longer before he turned back to his coworkers.

"You start a new workout routine, Declan? You've put on a lot of muscle lately," Amy observed as she worked with Emily to untangle a length of garland.

Rolling his shoulders so they wouldn't see his distress, Declan turned back and dramatically flexed first one bicep, then the other.

Everyone laughed. "Yes. Thank you for noticing, Amy," Declan said.

"Thank you for helping, everyone. I have to get to my 10:30 meeting, but I think our work here is done. Until Halloween, that is." Emily wiped her hands and smiled at Declan.

Emily left, and Declan continued to assist with the decorating. As they finished and packed the unused decorations back into the box, Mason asked the group, "Anyone up for lunch after this?"

Declan was about shake his head when he realized it might be the last time he'd break bread with this collection of humans. And maybe some protein would help him finish his report this afternoon.

He joined the chorus of responses. As they dispersed, Declan grabbed the box of decorations to return to the storage room. Mason said, "Let's head out at noon. I need to make sure my inbox isn't out of control before we leave. Meet in the lobby?"

"I'll swing by and see if Emily can join us. I think her meeting was only 30 minutes. See y'all soon." Amy waved to the group before turning and disappearing into a sea of uniform cubicles.

Declan walked to the storage room in a bit of a haze. He tried to soak in the details of the office, the drab wall color that didn't quite match the ugly commercial carpet.

He easily returned the box to the top shelf and looked around at all the storage clutter: pens that surely don't write any more, technology that is too old to function (floppy disk, anyone?).

Wolf shifters were fastidious about not collecting clutter as a general rule. When you live as long as a mated shifter does, a habit of holding onto physical items can quickly turn you into a hoarder.

It is also a great way to become out of sync with contemporary human culture. Supernaturals could either isolate and avoid humans entirely, or they could blend into human society to avoid detection. Blending required keeping up with the latest fashions and technology, not holding onto obsolete relics.

Returning to his cube, Declan was tempted to take off his shoes under his desk. His feet were rebelling at the confines of his leather loafers, which were now too small for his expanding feet. His wolf was also pawing at his insides. He definitely needed to shift and run after work; the large pack run during Saturday's full moon hadn't satisfied his wolf.

A delicate cough sounded from inside his cube. Declan flinched and swiveled around to see who was behind him. How could someone approach him without noticing? This level of distraction could be a fatal error for a predator like him. He needed to clear his head and focus.

"I hear you're joining us for lunch," Emily said as she sat down in the empty chair in his cube. "Before we head out, I wanted to talk to you about your slide deck on the air quality report. Got a minute?"

Declan smiled. His tiny human boss had always been kind to him, taking him under her wing to mentor. While he appreciated her efforts, he also found it amusing that she had no idea he was a crown prince, his wolf an alpha, and together they would rule the Tobin pack one day.

"Shoot." Declan grinned and gestured for her to continue.

"Your outline and sequence are great, but I think you could add a few more slides with some data to support your points a little better. Maybe at lunch you can ping Mason and he can help you with some data visualizations to add."

"Sure thing, that's a good idea. I'll talk to him at lunch and get a meeting on the books." Declan found it surprisingly hard to suppress a smile while talking to Emily. She was always thinking of ways to help him do better, learn more, and grow in his career.

She'd make a good queen, if she were a wolf.

But Emily was human, and no wolf had a human mate for at least two generations back. Maybe more. This must be another symptom of his impending twenty-fifth birthday. Could men suffer from raging hormones as they reached maturity?

A little more back and forth over his presentation prep, and then it was time for lunch. "I'll just go grab my purse, and we can head out." Emily stood and left his cube.

An hour later, and Amy, Mason, Emily, and Declan were sitting down at the chicken sandwich restaurant near their office. The fellowship was a balm to his wolf. Wolves were pack animals, and eating around a group of friends, even human ones, helped settle him somewhat.

"So, Declan, how was your weekend? Do anything to celebrate your birthday?" Mason asked around a mouthful of sandwich.

Declan shrugged. "Had a little party with some friends and family. It was fun. How was your weekend?"

"I built a spreadsheet to organize all my wife's book reviews. Nothing fancy, but she was super impressed. And grateful." Mason waggled his eyebrows then pushed his glasses back into place.

"Oh, you're gooood," Amy crooned. "Wish I had someone to organize my life like that." She sighed into her sandwich. "Emily, what are your plans for the weekend?"

"Isn't it a little early in the week to be asking about the weekend, Amy?" Emily teased.

"Only for you, Emily. You never have much to say about your weekend plans." Amy challenged Emily to share more than pleasantries about her weekend.

Declan was familiar with this exchange between the women. Amy was a very open personality, freely sharing details about her life outside of work. Whether or not the other person was interested.

In contrast, Emily was a closed book on anything personal. Reflecting on what he knew about her outside of work, Declan could inventory few details.

He was pretty sure she was single, lived alone, and was in her thirties. He knew she had a couple degrees in public health.

And that was about it.

He decided to chime in and goad her into revealing something personal. *Just to keep my mind distracted*, he reasoned.

Betrayal flashed across her face before Emily took the bait. "Here ya go: I'm going to New York City for the weekend. A little getaway. My flight is Thursday afternoon, and I took all day Thursday off in addition to Friday."

Emily's eyes brightened with her excitement. "Actually, not to talk shop at lunch, but Declan aren't you out the rest of the week, too? Don't forget to connect with Mason this afternoon on that presentation." Emily weaponized her French fry to emphasize her point.

Declan used his own fry to salute her in return. Nice deflection, Em. "Yes ma'am. Mason, I'll grab you as soon as we're back, if you're free."

"That works. You're out the next couple of days? I didn't know that. Doing anything fun?" Mason asked Declan.

"Yes and no. I'm taking some personal time for my birthday tomorrow and doing family stuff Wednesday and Thursday. Just figured I'd make it easy and take the days off. I'll be back Friday." Declan looked at his food as he spoke.

"You do a lot with your family," Amy observed. "I think it is sweet. Must make your mom thrilled. Mine is constantly complaining I don't call her enough. But when I do call, all she talks about is how I don't visit enough. Gah, drives me nuts." Everyone laughed as Amy rolled her eyes dramatically.

Lunch continued in companionable chitchat, and luckily no one asked Declan about his plans for the week. He didn't like lying to them, and there wasn't a human equivalent to *I'm about to learn the name of my fated mate and begin searching for her.*

He also didn't want to resign his human employment under a cloud of mystery. He liked these humans, and he sincerely enjoyed the years that he had worked with them. But like all the other males in his pack, his exposure to human society would end on his twenty-fifth birthday, when his focus would return to living, working, and supporting the pack while also beginning the search for his mate.

Yes, he was procrastinating. He put in for vacation the rest of this week instead of just quitting today. He would pop back into the office Friday to give his notice. He might even give them two weeks, as was the human custom.

"You seem really pensive. Everything okay?" Emily patted his shoulder as they walked back into the office. He smiled down at her look of care and concern. She was a really lovely person. Beautiful inside and out, with curves that made him long to unwrap her to discover what she was hiding behind all her cardigans and pencil skirts. He would wrap her silky blonde hair around his fist...

What was he doing?

Those were entirely inappropriate thoughts to have about one's boss. He needed to get a grip or his hormones would have him dry humping the bushes next.

Thankfully, the elevator saved him at that moment. "I'm fine, thanks for checking Emily. I appreciate you." He gave her his best megawatt smile and gestured for her to precede him into the elevator with Amy and Mason. "I think I'll take the stairs though, work off all that fried chicken I ate at lunch." He let the door close before she could protest.

Declan didn't want to be trapped with her and Amy's scent in a small space. Hell, at this rate, he probably shouldn't be in a confined space with Mason either.

He challenged his wolf to run up the stairs the whole way to the sixth floor. He needed to burn off his restless energy. Just a few more hours and his work day would be over. Finish the report, meet with Mason on the data, then he could go home and let his wolf run. His wolf pranced at the idea of a good run in the forest.

He put all thoughts of what would change tomorrow into a box inside his mind. *Just focus on getting through today,* he told himself.

One more day to be free of the burdens of a mate.

CHAPTER 3

T he next evening, Declan entered his parents' kitchen. His mother was bustling around, and his sister was doing her best to help get dinner ready without becoming roadkill.

"Hey, Mom," Declan said.

"Hello, Declan. Happy birthday. Dinner is almost ready. Why don't you see if your father needs anything?" Elaine said while both stirring a saucepan on the stovetop and running her index finger down the page of a recipe book.

Theodora rolled her eyes and smiled at him. He might be the future alpha of the pack, but no one was above getting dismissed by the queen.

With a salute, Declan followed orders and soon located his father in the home office, sharing a drink with Jack.

"Hiding I see," Declan greeted the pair.

"Safety in numbers, son. Your mother is very excited about this evening, and I think she's pouring all her energy into the meal. She hasn't cooked like this since..." King Theo paused, swirled his whiskey, then shrugged. "I actually can't remember the last time she went into a kitchen frenzy like this. You should feel special. Happy birthday, son."

Jack mirrored his grin. "Drink for the birthday boy?" He held up the crystal decanter half full of amber liquid.

"Sure," Declan replied.

"So, how's your head, son? Are you ready to learn her name tonight?" Theo returned to his deck chair and leaned back.

Shrugging, Declan took the drink from his brother's hand and sat on the end of the leather couch opposite the sturdy wooden desk where his father completed vital pack business.

Jack and Theo simultaneously raised their eyebrows at his nonchalant response. He smoothed his blue jeans down his muscular thighs, procrastinating from having to voice the emotions he'd been squashing since yesterday.

"Well, at this point, I'm just ready to get it over with. Is the Seer eating dinner with us, or is she arriving later to do my reading?" Declan looked to Theo for the answers.

"Finding your mate is not something to get over with, son. Tonight, you begin the most important task of your entire, and hopefully long, life. Why do you dread it?" Theo's posture continued to be relaxed, leaning back and sipping his drink.

But his eye contact was intense. The besotted king grew serious any time the subject of mates came up. His love for his queen was legendary among his pack, and he never missed an opportunity to share his intensity on the topic.

Jack was keenly observing the interaction from his silent half of the couch. He was only a couple of years younger than Declan, but his twenty-fifth was just around the corner. Try as he might to appear disinterested, Jack was taking mental notes.

"I'm not dreading it, exactly. My wolf has just been… insufferable lately. And I'm all uncomfortable. Both in my body and in my mind. I had the weirdest thoughts about a coworker yesterday. I'm ready to feel like myself again." Declan scratched his scalp at the memory.

"Yes, there is a period of uncomfortable transition as your body finally matures in preparation for mating. I know how uncomfortable it can be, but it'll pass as soon as you find her." Theo nodded his head as if his words had the power to make it so.

"You mean, *if* he finds her. Just look at Killian," Jack chimed in.

There was a moment of silence as they all contemplated the situation of the top pack enforcer, Killian. He was ten years older than Declan, but he had been a close friend of the family ever since his father died when Killian was a young teenager. Now, Declan and Killian were best friends.

Killian was still looking for his mate at thirty-five. The Seer told him her name, as was custom, but he had yet to find her. The loneliness was beginning to wear on him, and the entire family felt for him.

"No good comes from worrying about problems that don't exist yet," Theo interrupted their thoughts. "Why don't you try to focus on the positive aspects? What are you looking forward to the most?"

Declan tried and failed to think of an answer. What were the positives?

One person, forever.

No choice in who that person would be.

No second chances if you can't work it out with that person.

"How do you make it work?" Declan asked.

"Work? With your mother?" Theo wrinkled his brows in confusion.

"Yeah. You both always seemed disgustingly happy. All the time. Did you ever, I dunno, mix it up a little? Keep things fresh and interesting?" Declan hated to ask, but he needed to know. Time was running out for him to ask these questions before everything changed.

"Fresh and interesting?" Theo echoed. "Son, you're asking the wrong questions. You don't keep things 'fresh' or 'interesting' with your mate. You worry how you're going to breathe when she's not in the room."

Jack and Declan silently digested their father's words. Theo sipped his whiskey and glanced at the door to his office. Almost like he was contemplating going to his mate right at that moment.

Is that really how it is with your fated mate? Is it like that every time?

Before Theo could respond, Theodora entered the office without preamble. "I need a drink."

Laughing, Theo rose to pour her a whiskey mixed heavily with ginger beer. "Your mother running you ragged? I appreciate you volunteering to help her."

"A life decision I now regret. I can't wait to return to school." Accepting her drink, she looked at Declan. "I hope you appreciate my noble sacrifice. I'm missing two days of lectures only to become a kitchen slave. She's wound so tight, you'd think she was on the verge of learning her own mates name, not her son's."

"But is it ready yet? I'm hungry. And Dad never answered my question. Is the Seer coming for dinner or arriving after?" Declan rose and followed Theodora out of the office.

"Yes, it's ready. No, the Seer isn't eating with us. She'll

arrive at 7:30 for your reading." Theodora took a long sip of her cocktail as they rounded the corner into the dining room.

Theo made a beeline to his mate, kissing her with the passion felt by a couple separated for years, not mere hours. Gripping her hips possessively, he said, "Dinner looks exquisite. Thank you for the hard work in putting it all together. Expect to be rewarded later."

Elaine blushed at the last bit, which was murmured more than said. Still loud enough for the kids to hear and all of them groaned in unison. She laughed and placed her hand on his cheek briefly, in the way longtime mates show casual affection.

Taking seats and beginning the process of passing dishes and filling plates, Theo cleared his throat.

"Today is a big day for us, Elaine. Our firstborn is about to learn the name of his mate. And begin the most important task he will ever take on." His eyes shimmered as his gaze bored straight into his queen.

"I just hope she likes us as much as I know we will love her," Elaine said to the table at large.

"Mom, let's slow down here. He might not find her right away. Or she might want live somewhere else. Or she might be awful. Don't get your hopes up." Theodora's attempts to settle her mother's anxiousness backfired by triggering a cascade of worst-case scenarios.

Sensing his mate's distress, Theo interjected, "Theodora, that is enough. These details do not matter. We will embrace the mate that Fate has chosen for Declan. And we will adapt as we learn more about her. Just because we don't know everything yet, doesn't mean we know it will be bad. It could just as easily be good. Don't—"

"—fear the unknown, just embrace it." Declan, Jack, and Theodora finished his familiar phrase for him.

Laughing, Theo raised his hands in surrender. "Okay, okay. So you know what I'm going to say. Clever. Now why don't y'all try to live by it for a change?"

Declan couldn't help but smile. His family was full of love, and they clearly enjoyed each other. Not that he'd admit that to his siblings, of course. But reflecting on his childhood, their home was always filled with love and joy.

He also couldn't remember a time without his siblings. What would it be like to introduce an entirely new person into their family unit? How would the dynamics change?

A gentle hand squeezed his. Looking up from his plate, he saw that his mother could sense his mood. She didn't say anything, just gave him another squeeze and a smile in support.

"Whatever comes, Declan, we will make it work. You leave the worrying to me. Just focus on finding her quickly. I can't wait to meet her."

The rest of dinner blissfully focused on other topics. Theodora's college classes. Jack's military training. He could sense a collective endeavor to keep the conversation lighthearted and focused anywhere but on him.

Declan felt another wave of gratitude for his family when the doorbell rang. Elaine, Theodora, and Jack began cleaning all the empty dishes from the table, while Theo went to answer the door. Before he left the dining room, he called over his shoulder, "After the table is cleared, Elaine and Theodora, don't lift a finger with the dishes. Do you hear me, Jack?"

A prompt yet grumbled "yes, sir" rang out from the kitchen.

Declan found himself at a loss of what to do. Should he

retreat to the kitchen and wait to be summoned? Should he stay put and greet the Seer when she entered? He compromised by doing neither, and just paced the perimeter of the dining room with his hands in his blue jean pockets.

A few minutes later, a woman wearing an elaborate costume entered the room. She was carrying some sort of antique satchel with folding wooden legs, almost like an old-timey sewing bag.

But the real show stopper was her headdress. The turban was ordained with a wide assortment of objects, from jewels to antlers, to animal bones. Declan squinted— were those teeth sewn on one side?

A large trio of peacock feathers extended from the center jewel of a headband she wore across her forehead. It was unclear if the headband was a separate item or just another piece of accoutrements with the headdress. Her eyelids were dramatic with dark eye shadow and bold eyeliner. Red lipstick popped against her bright white teeth.

She wore a flowing dress that looked like a cross between a muumuu and a kaftan. It was also dark with a gradient of colors from black to grey to off-white.

A large hand came down on his shoulder, followed by an unpleasantly firm squeeze. "Remember your manners, son," Theo growled directly into his ear.

Reaching maturity might make certain aspects of his life go all topsy-turvy, but apparently some things would never change.

"Thank you for coming, Seer. It is an honor to have you visit me this evening." Declan extended his hand for a shake, but the Seer did not reciprocate. She simply hummed her response and began making herself comfortable at the head of the table.

Declan was about to correct her that it was the king's seat, but Theo discretely grabbed his elbow.

"Please make yourself comfortable, Seer. My mate will be here momentarily with the boiling water." Theo gestured for Declan to sit next to her, and he took the seat on her other side.

The Seer did not waste any time setting up her odd satchel, opening it so that the wooden legs kicked out to suspend the fabric bag.

She took out an assortment of items with practiced efficiency. By the time Elaine entered with an electric kettle full of boiling water, the Seer was ready for her.

"In the teapot, please, my Queen." The Seer finally spoke her first words.

"You honor us with your presence, Seer," Elaine responded as she poured the hot water over the tea strainer full of loose tea leaves. Declan discretely shivered as he anticipated the surely awful taste of whatever concoction she was brewing for him.

Elaine took a seat beside Theo, and Jack and Theodora silently filled in the remaining seats.

No one spoke. The Seer was the only one comfortable with the silence. Everyone else, the king and queen included, fidgeted.

Relying on experience, without any type of visible timer, the Seer determined the tea had steeped long enough. She poured six teacups of the brew, handing one to each member of the family in a deliberate manner.

When no one moved, the Seer lifted a hand with multiple rings and said, "Well, what are you waiting for? Drink."

The family moved as one to take the first sip. "Oh, this tastes like Earl Grey," Theodora said.

"Yes, it is my favorite. I enjoy the bergamot flavor," The Seer replied.

Declan stifled a chuckle. She might appear eccentric, but the pack Seer had a normal side too, it would seem.

As he continued to sip his tea, he wondered how old she was. With the headdress and heavy makeup, it was hard to tell. But her skin was flawless and smooth. For the first time, Declan found himself curious about the female everyone knew as the pack's clairvoyant. She was a wolf shifter and lived in a cottage just outside of downtown Howling Forest. But that was about all Declan—or anyone else—knew about her.

"Give me your cup." Her voice broke through his musings, and he suddenly realized his cup was nearly empty.

Handing his teacup over, the tension in the room began to ramp up. He could hear his mother's rapid breathing. Declan's own heart began to pound louder and faster with each passing moment as the Seer swirled his teacup first one direction, then the other.

Suddenly, her hand flared out and made a dramatic circle. The teacup ended its journey with a flick of her wrist to distribute the leaves evenly across a special mat she had unrolled before her.

A fly's fart could have been heard in that room while the family studied the Seer as she studied his tea leaves.

Tense minutes passed. The Seer rotated the mat this way and that, inspecting the leaves from every angle. Her face was expressionless except for the corners of her eyes, which crinkled as she read whatever message Fate wrote in the remnants of his teacup.

Finally, she frowned before straightening up. Declan

was not prepared for the first time she gave him direct eye contact.

"Your mate's name is Sabine Valentine, and she is in danger. There is a threat to her life that is close to her lifeline. You need to find her soon." The Seer then reached over and grabbed his hand. "Find her and protect her, Declan. Your mate is important."

ABOUT THE AUTHOR

Dive into the passionate world of Beth DeWeese, where steamy paranormal romance comes to life and ignites the page. Beth writes irresistible love stories that help readers escape from reality with love and adventure.

Beth's novels are a blend of smoldering chemistry, pulse-pounding action, and heartfelt tenderness. Her stories feature irresistibly sexy heroes and fierce, independent heroines who discover not just love, but their own inner strength as they navigate the tumultuous waters of romance.

When she's not crafting delightful love stories, Beth is living out her own happily-ever-after in Franklin, Tennessee (USA). She shares a home filled with laughter, love, and a pack of adorable canine companions with her real-life hero – her husband.